DORI'S GIFT

Angie Wilson

Illustrated by Ashley Teets

Use your gifts for Good Things

[signature: Angie Wilson]

[signature: Ashley Teets]

Headline Kids
an imprint of Headline Books, Inc.
Terra Alta, WV

Dori's Gift

by Angie Wilson
illustrated by Ashley Teets

copyright ©2014 Angie Wilson

To order additional copies of this book, for book publishing information, or to contact the author:

Headline Books, Inc.
P.O. Box 52, Terra Alta, WV 26764
www.HeadlineKids.com

Tel: 800-570-5951
Email: mybook@headlinebooks.com

Headline Kids is an imprint of Headline Books

ISBN-13: 978-0-938467-85-4

Library of Congress Control Number: 2013951214

Wilson, Angie
      Dori's gift /Angie Wilson
      p. cm.
      ISBN 978-0-938467-85-4
      1. Appalachia 2. Appalachian heritage 3. Family 4. Dulcimer

It's Dori's birthday and she wonders what her gift will be. She doesn't have to do all her chores on her special day but pitches in anyway. This is a wonderful story of pioneer living and one in a series of "Appalachian Heritage."

PRINTED IN THE UNITED STATES OF AMERICA

Dedicated to:
For my mom, Joyce Thompson Whitlow, who grew up
in a musical family and passed the gift on to me.

Acknowledgments:
To Jesus, for His unending mercy and grace.

To my husband, Derek, for his love and support
during the long process of getting published.

To my children and grandchildren who inspire me
and I hope that somehow I will inspire them.

To Aunt Becky, a treasure in the Thompson family
that is cherished by all.

Special thanks to:
Cathy Teets, Headline Books,
for helping this dream to come true.

Ashley Teets for her beautiful artwork
and for being patient in this process.

Samuel R. Sink for his vision and support.

"Breakfast is ready," yelled a voice outside the bedroom door. Dori opened her eyes and realized her sisters and roommates, Ruth and Becky, were gone. She took this rare opportunity to stretch her legs and arms as far as she could reach across the bed. She loved the way the quilts felt heavy on her body; she loved the smell of coffee and bacon mingled together. She loved mornings. Dori wondered briefly why she was allowed to miss the morning chores, for she knew she wasn't sick. Then she remembered—*it was her birthday, she turned seven today!*

5

She closed her eyes and wondered if she would receive a gift. Mama always made their birthdays special, but the last two years had been dry summers and the crops were low so the children had not received a gift. Birthdays were still good days at her house, for Mama always baked a cake and made their favorite meal on their special day.

Dori opened her eyes and looked around the room. There were many things she was thankful for—her clothes, her doll, and the books on the shelf. She felt bad for wanting more, because she and her siblings were blessed with more than many of their friends. She closed her eyes again and prayed a prayer of thankfulness for all her blessings, and then she jumped out of bed.

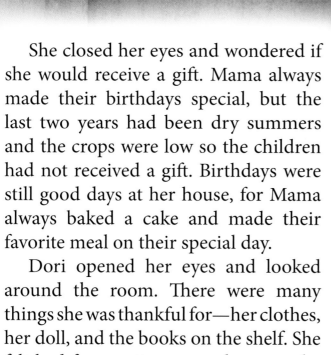

Dori's warm feet hit the cold wooden floor, and she ran downstairs as fast as she could to Mama's warm stove. The warmth of the fire quickly eased the chill of the brisk November morning. She stretched her fingers out, and cautiously held them as close to the stove as she could get. The stove was piping hot, and although it was her favorite place to be on frigid mornings, she had felt the consequences of getting too close. As she stood there, lost in the warmth of the fire, she didn't hear her brother, Cecil, sneaking up behind her with a finger full of butter for the birthday girl's nose.

Laughter quickly filled the house at the sight of Dori's greasy face.

Dori promptly cleaned her face, ate breakfast, combed her hair and got dressed. Today was Monday, "wash day," the hardest working day for Dori and her sisters. Her three older brothers headed out to school, but the girls did not go to school on wash day because there was too much work to be done at home. She heard Papa outside working on the fire in the wash house and getting the kettle ready, so she quickly bounded down the stairs and raced Ruth and Becky to the springhouse. Ruth, the youngest, always got the smallest bucket, but it was a battle between Dori and Becky for the medium-sized bucket. Once again Becky came in first, and Dori was stuck toting the large bucket.

13

The girls worked all morning filling and refilling the kettle and wash tub with rain water from the barrel on the porch, and making sure there was plenty of homemade lye soap in the tub as well.

The clothes were transported from the kettle to the tub to be scrubbed on a washboard, then back to the kettle and stirred with a stick to rinse. The white clothes were boiled and hung on the clothesline while the towels and work clothes were thrown across the fence.

Mama did the scrubbing, and the girls helped with the rest of the tasks. Dori loved to listen to Mama as she sang while she worked. The tunes varied from lively folk songs to hymns. Some of her favorites were "Soldier's Boy," "Little Maggie," and "Unclouded Day." Dori's fingers ached from the cool fall air contrasting with the steaming hot clothes, but by mid-afternoon, the washing was over.

The girls worked feverishly all day. Dori and her sisters had a little time to play before supper. Without delay they transformed the outhouse into a cute little playhouse. They spread a quilt over the toilet hole, and added pillows and dolls. There were times they hosted fancy tea parties in their "playhouse." Dori knew Mama would take the time out of her busy day to share at least one cup of tea.

It was getting close to suppertime, and Dori was getting very excited. She knew Mama would fix her favorite meal on her birthday. Her mouth watered as she thought of fried tenderloin, potatoes fried with onions, and hot cornbread. Soon Mama rang the old cowbell that hung by the kitchen door, which notified the family that it was time to eat.

"Do you think you'll get a gift today?" Ruth asked Dori as they were washing their hands in the washtub on the porch.

"I don't know, I've been thinking about it all day," Dori replied.

"What do you think you'll get?"

"Maybe a doll, or a new dress."

"I hope it's not a pair of high-heeled shoes," Ruth teased. The girls laughed at the thought of Becky, who once received a pair of high-heeled shoes. Becky loved the shoes, and insisted on wearing them to Sunday school, even though the family walked two miles to church. Becky's feet ached for days after that grueling walk.

As soon as supper was over, Papa rose from the table and told Dori to close her eyes. Ruth closed her eyes, too, for she was just as eager. Papa placed a medium-sized wooden box in front of her. Excitement filled the air as she opened her eyes and saw the gift.

23

She gently ran her hand over the lid of the box. The box had musical notes carved on the lid with Dori's name in the center. She knew Papa made this gift in his workshop. Was this why he had been spending so much time in the shop lately? She felt this was a special gift, and she savored every moment of this occasion.

When she could stand it no more, she delicately unhooked the latch and opened the box. Resting inside was the most magnificent dulcimer Dori had ever seen. It was made of dark stained wood that glistened with a glossy coat. There were two roses engraved on it, and four strings wound tightly at the neck.

She closed her eyes and held the dulcimer as she whispered a prayer of thanks. This was the greatest gift she had ever seen. She sat frozen in her chair—afraid to move for fear of waking up and discovering this was only a dream. Her fears vanished as she gently touched each string. Her small hand fit comfortably around the neck as she lifted the gift and held it close to her. The quiet hush of the moment was broken as Dori strummed a chord.

The family cheered at this joyful sound, and each of her many siblings started requesting songs for her to play. She already knew how to play three chords, which enabled her to play many simple tunes. She had watched her older brothers, Cecil and Buddy, play many times. They had patiently taken the time to teach her a few chords. It was because of this interest Papa decided to make this gift. They were a musical family and they tried to nurture the talent of each child. Papa smiled as he looked at Dori, for he knew that part of the gift could not be held in her hands. The love of music had been silently given to her as it had been given to him and to his parents by God, a musical heritage that extends to each generation.

Once again, Dori sat in front of the stove—except this time she was not warming her hands, but the hearts of her family as she played her dulcimer and they all sang together in sweet harmony.

29

There's a land that is fairer than day,
And by faith we can see it afar;
For the Father waits over the way,
To prepare us a dwelling place there.
In the sweet by-and-by,
We shall meet on that beautiful shore;
In the sweet by-and-by,
We shall meet on that beautiful shore.

This was the happiest day of Dori's childhood, and her most memorable birthday. She would continue to play and sing for her family, neighbors and friends on many occasions. Her beautiful voice would echo through their tiny country church for years, blessing many people at Sunday services, weddings and special occasions. Dori's gift would fill the hills, hollows and hearts of her people for many, many years.

Appalachian people were hardworking and self-reliant. They farmed the rugged terrain, and through hard labor produced crops. There wasn't much that came easy to them, so their possessions were cherished and they thanked God for His provision and for meeting their needs. The Appalachian worked from dawn to dusk, but found time to enjoy life as well. Neighbors would join together to make tasks more enjoyable such as making molasses or apple butter, killing hogs, shelling beans and husking corn. These events would finish with a big dinner that the host family provided and usually would come to an end with singing and storytelling.

"Appalachia" is a word that often evokes images of sullen, depressing lives. The region is full of rural areas that are prone to poverty, and thus it is often painted as a picture of hopelessness. Rugged mountain ranges have isolated the people and formed barriers to the modernization of society. There are some parts of the region where the remoteness held traditions for many years from Ireland, Scotland, England and Germany—everything from songs, home remedies, and crafts to unique words and phrases in their language. These traditions were carried into the mountains by the settlers and remained there, untainted from the changing world.

Dori's Gift is a story that shows the reader a glimpse of the history and tradition of the region with ties to the Scots-Irish settlers. The Appalachian Mountains are filled with a colorful culture of arts and crafts that demonstrate the talent and perseverance of a strong people. They are prone to be self-sufficient and take pride in their creations; from basket-weaving, quilting, pottery, and furniture-making to crafting instruments that liven up their ballads and hymns. These proved to be key to their survival as a people. One such instrument is the dulcimer, which is common in Appalachia. Its origin can be traced back to the Bible, in fact, some people say that in many regions, the mountain people would only use instruments that are in the Bible, which explains why the dulcimer was so widely accepted. The dulcimer was very inexpensive to make and became popular for that reason as well.

The Appalachian home was filled with music and singing, and many of the ballads held ties to their Scots-Irish roots. Most of the old songs were not written down, but were orally passed from one generation to the next. The women would often sing while they worked. The children grew to love the hymns and ballads and passed them on to the next generation. Many of the old Irish songs told of Lords and Ladies from their homeland far away. Some of the songs changed through the years and places in Ireland were changed to local towns. One example is the song "Barbara Allen," which has been rewritten many times to include places in Appalachia.